Deegee

Deegee

the Corgi

By Joann Song

Illustrations by Natalie Loseva

Printed in the United States of America

ISBN 978-1-953910-13-4 (hardcover)
ISBN 978-1-953910-14-1 (paperback)
ISBN 978-1-953910-35-6 (e-book)

Canoe Tree Press
4697 Main Street
Manchester Center, VT 05255

Canoe Tree Press is a division of DartFrog Books.

To my family, S.O, Deegee, Yuna...
... and all the little ones who brought
us joy during a difficult year.

Sniff-sniff-sniff, I go between the cardboard boxes. They are mostly full of dusty books and clothes.

Yesterday, Jessica came home with all her boxes and brought them back to this room. Her school "shut down," she said. She's staying home for a while.

Jessica's brother, Dave, stopped going to school, too. He is a student at "You See LA," a college close to home. Dave would ride a red motorbike to school. And now it's gone. The other day, a stranger came up to the driveway and met Dave downstairs. I started barking at the man. He handed Dave something and took his keys. Then, he left with the red motorbike and never returned. It made a loud "Vroom! Vroom!" noise as he sped off.

So much has changed this year. The neighborhood feels different. It's much quieter. Children are not playing outside. Sidewalks and streets are empty.

Jessica is sitting on her bed and paging through a photo album. I jump on top of her bed and cuddle next to her. She opens up the album to the first page and says, "This is when you joined the family."

Together, we take a stroll down memory corgi lane.

The Lee family adopted me when I was a pup. It happened so quickly. One moment, I'm walking out of the apartment I was born in. Next, I'm in a Toyota Sienna with five strangers. Together, we drove to Los Angeles.

I was scared, but their warm energy made me feel better.
They are good humans. I am safe.

My first human named me "Dee-Oh-Gee."

The Lee family liked "Deegee" better,
so now that's my name.

Days and weeks passed slowly. Memories of my first
home faded. I understood that he would not return.
And each day, my bond with the Lees grew stronger.

This is my home. They are my family.

My new home is nice and cozy. We live on the second-story of a bright, yellow house. Another family lives below us. Sometimes, they get all fussy when I bark at night. I can hear them yelling from downstairs. This makes me bark even louder.

There are three bedrooms in the house: one each for Jessica and Dave and one for the parents. I'm usually curled up on the couch, listening to the busy sounds on the streets: children playing, cars honking, loud sirens, neighbors yelling, and dogs barking.

13

SUMMER 2018

Julie is standing next to me in these bright, sunny photos. Here we are at the beach, one of our many adventures. I love going to the beach. I like sinking my paws in the sand and running away from the waves before they swallow me whole.

We have so much fun. I never know where we'll end up when I hop inside the car. As soon as I smell the ocean breeze, I get so excited.

Right now, I am half covered in Jessica's warm blanket. It reminds me of the summer's radiant heat.

I sigh with longing for all the happy times. I close my eyes and I'm back on the beach.

Let me tell you more about Julie. She's the oldest Lee sibling. She lives with her husband in a different home. We used to spend a lot of time together, before everything turned weird. Julie and I love to practice tricks and she spoils me with treats.

My favorite trick is when she points at me with two fingers and goes, "Bang! Bang!" And I fall to my side.

Bang! Bang!

I get extra treats for that one.

The sheep herding class
was another fun adventure.
I even made friends with
other corgis! First, we
each got to chase after a
few goats. That part was
easy. Then, they brought out
the sheep. *Silly sheep*. I dashed after
them and zig-zagged between their legs.
You should have seen me. Let me tell you, I was born to do this. I
knew exactly what to do. It was my first time in the class, and I
passed with flying colors. The lady called me a "very smart corgi."

I guess corgis *are* special. Not every dog can pass
this class. Julie was so proud of me.

At the end of the summer the house became a lot quieter. That was when Jessica, the youngest Lee, left home for college. I napped on her bed while she packed her boxes. Papa Lee and her brother helped her move. I watched from the window as they drove off together in the Toyota Sienna. Jessica's school, "You See San Diego," is far from home. That meant she couldn't visit us that often.

I would rest in her empty room, sniffing her blankets and lying on the carpet. At night, I waited for Dave. When I heard the rumbling sound of his motorbike. I'd know he was home.

My ears perk up when Dave sticks his head inside Jessica's room and asks, "You want to go to McDonald's?" Jessica nods eagerly and closes the album. Dave and Jessica like to stay up watching shows and eating fast food. I get to ride in the backseat of the car as they go to the drive thru. I can smell the salty fries from a mile away. Jessica likes getting fries and dipping them in ice cream.

I sit close to the coffee table, inches away from the food. If I'm lucky, I'll find a few lonely fries that have fallen to the floor. Or I'll stick my snout inside the 'M' bag and savor the salty aroma. *Ah, that heavenly smell.*

I am floating on a cloud today. A thick, smoky cloud. Mama Lee is frying meat in the kitchen. I follow her around while she prepares dinner. I stand too close to her feet and I yelp when she accidentally steps on my paws.

Mama Lee cooks most of the meals for the family. That's how she shows her love. Tonight she is cooking ribs. I wag my tail and patiently wait, hoping (begging) to try a piece of the wonderful smelling meat. It has a sweet scent that I love.

She shakes her head and says, "Kalbi is not for you, Deegee."

Instead, she feeds me rice and chicken. It's not as juicy, but I enjoy it.

The front door goes click and I run down
the stairs. Papa Lee is home from work.

Humans have to go to work to get money. They need
money for food, treats, cars, and more food. If the
Lees didn't work, then we wouldn't have this home.
They wouldn't be able to feed me rice and chicken.

Papa Lee is very tired when he's done with work. He is
covered in grease and dirt. After washing up, he takes
his dinner to his room and eats it in front of the TV. I
follow him inside and stare at him until he gives me
a bite. *Mm, kalbi tastes even better than I thought.*

Dave gets mad when he catches
Papa Lee sharing his food.

"She can't eat that," he says sternly.

Papa Lee pulls his hand away and I
quickly scurry out of the room.

Jessica is talking on the phone and loudly pressing keys on her laptop. I peer inside. She seems anxious.

"It's not working. What should I do? Nothing is open right now." She says, "Ok, I'll come over," and slams the laptop shut.

I walk over to her and she smiles at me. She kneels down and gently gives me a kiss on the head. I feel better. She seems to feel better too.

Jessica is gone for the rest of the night. I fall asleep on the couch, waiting for her to return. I open my eyes as soon as I hear the door open and footsteps softly climbing up the stairs. I can only see shadows, but I smell Jessica's floral perfume and fall back asleep.

The next day, Dave and Jessica are turning the living room upside down, looking for his keys.

Jessica lifts the cushions and says, "It was here this morning."

I remember something falling off the couch. I heard a small thud when it hit the ground. I stick my snout and front paws in the dark space underneath. It doesn't reach very far.

Dave chuckles and says, "Deegee, you can't fit." They lift and move the couch.

Jessica reaches in the gap and exclaims, "There it is!"

She picks up a dirty sock and hands Dave the keys. I see a lonely french fry. I squeeze in the opening and quickly snatch it up.

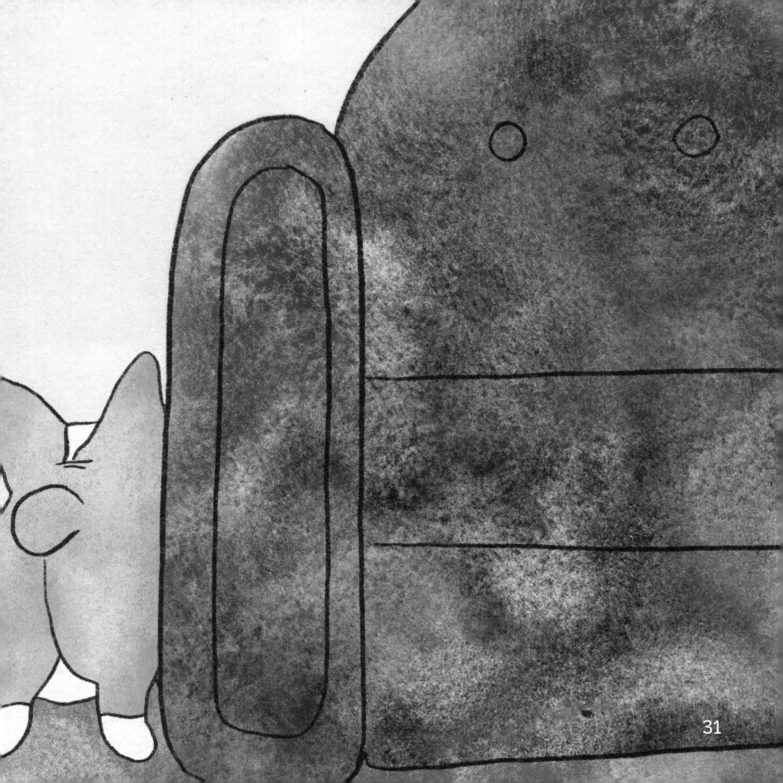

BIRTHDAY

I learned to count to twelve by staring
at the round clock everyday.

One-zero is *ten*.
One-one is *eleven*.
One-two is *twelve*.

The time is close to five. I hear footsteps.
I dash downstairs to the door and wag my tail.

33

Julie swings the door open and sings, "Deegee, I'm home!" Her voice echoes like ripples in a pond.

She's home for *my* birthday. I'm so excited. I almost knock over the cake when I jump up to give her a sloppy kiss. Dave follows close behind and playfully chases after me.

I zip back and forth from the kitchen to the hallway. *Oh boy, today is a great day.* Jessica throws a ball down the hallway. I eagerly fetch it and bring it back to her. Julie hands me a treat and leads me to the couch.

I do a few more circles around the living room and dining table. All my humans are finally home again.

For dinner, we all wear silly triangle hats and sing "Happy Birthday." I start howling and singing along with the high notes: "Awoooo!" This makes them laugh.

My cake looks like a big bone, but it tastes like peanut butter and bread. It's tasty and chewy. I lick the plate clean instantly. My belly feels like it is going to burst. I roll over on the floor and breathe slowly.

Best birthday ever

The Lee siblings gather in the living room afterwards. They keep saying "jump," but I don't feel like jumping. I turn my head towards them. They are facing the TV. Maybe they're saying "chomp?" I lift one ear so I can hear them better.

They are talking about a man. *Trump. I heard that name before.* He lives in a big white house far away from here and gives humans orders from the TV. The siblings say he is doing bad things. He sounds like a bad person. The kind that you bark at when they enter the house or get close to you.

They start talking about something else and turn on a show.

Their laughter makes me feel calm. I soon drift off to sleep.

DIET

I am in a blue, oversized bag. Dave is balancing me on a scale. I'm standing on my hind legs and trying to jump out. Papa Lee is watching us.

He walks over and says to Dave, "No. Hold Deegee. Then, minus your weight."

I'm freed from the bag. Dave carries me and steps on the scale. Then, he lets me go and steps on it again.

He looks down and shakes his head.

"Deegee needs to go on a diet."

Oh. That doesn't sound good.

Pizza boxes are stacked on the dinner table.
Dirty clothes and dishes are slowly piling up.

Mama Lee has been sleeping a lot lately.
She is cooking less too. Instead of chicken
and rice, I've only been eating kibbles.

I hear a loud rumbling in the living room. Dave is gliding the vacuum back and forth. It hurts my ears.

This thing is my enemy. I dash in front of it and start growling and barking. *I'm not afraid of you, vacuum.*

Suddenly, it is quiet again. The evil vacuum stops moving. Dave drags me to his room and closes the door. I am stuck inside. And the rumbling continues.

I have to stop it!

43

The rumbling in the living room drowns out my anxious cries for help. There is nothing I can do.

Soon, the noise stops, and Dave opens the bedroom door. I am released from captivity. We have defeated the vacuum. And I woke up Mama Lee.

She slowly walks over to the kitchen and turns on the stove. The sound and smell of sizzling meat fills our home.

The family is gathered in front of the TV with their arms crossed. These days, the Lees are all very tense. They look very worried. I can hear them talking a lot about "Corona." It's a virus. It's in the air and it's spreading. No one can see it, because it's very small. It can hurt humans and make them very sick. Especially older ones, like Mama and Papa Lee. They are afraid. They always shield their faces when we go for walks. I think it protects them from the bad, invisible thing.

I wonder if I can get Corg-ona. *Do I need a mask, too?*

I feel restless. I run circles around the house and dash up and down the stairs.

Jessica yells over the TV, "Stop it, Deegee."

I want to go outside. The house is starting to feel smaller. I miss running around freely and playing with my friends at the park. Especially my pal, Homer. We're about the same size so we get along great. He even has the same brown and white coat as me. We like to chase each other and see who can catch the ball first. Our moms met at the park. It's been a long time since we've played together. I miss being around my friends.

Julie doesn't spend as much time with us anymore. She came by a few days ago to drop off food. I gave her a sloppy kiss. Julie hugged me and Jessica, but she didn't hug Mama and Papa Lee. She didn't even come inside. It was strange. They stood far apart as they talked. Then, she drove away.

Papa Lee doesn't go to work lately. He doesn't say much, but I can feel his sadness. I rest next to his feet and keep him company. Mama and Papa Lee have been arguing a lot. I don't know what they're saying, but I don't like it when they yell. I usually hide in Jessica or Dave's room.

Last night, Jessica left the house after dinner. Mama Lee snapped at her when she returned.

"Where did you go? Don't leave the house."

Jessica snapped back, "I just went for a drive by myself!" And then she locked herself in her room. She only opened it to let me in after I scratched at her door.

49

The good thing is, they're home all day. Dave and Jessica are usually in their rooms studying. Even though we don't play as much, I'm happy to spend time with them. At night, we all hang out in the living room. Bags of chips and bowls of ice cream are piled on the coffee table. They don't share any of it with me. I huff at them, but they don't notice. They keep stuffing their greedy faces.

The man on TV is talking about dogs. This year, many dogs are finding forever homes. He says shelters are empty. We are helping humans during the lockdown. I hope they all find a family like the Lees.

Dave rubs my head and says to Jessica, "What would we do without Deegee?"

"I don't know," she responds. "Deegee is the best."

BRIGHTER

Mama Lee is back
from the market.
She's carrying bags of
groceries inside from her
Sienna. I stick my snout
in one of the bags.
It's a jar of spicy
cabbage. The Lees
like to eat this.
I can't eat spicy food.
The smell is too strong.
It burns my nose and
makes my eyes water.

I'm now surrounded by
groceries and a wall of toilet paper. *So much toilet
paper.* I weasel my way out of the kitchen.

Mama Lee is singing. It's been a while since I've heard
her sing. Her voice is lovely and soothing.

Dave asks Jessica, "Did you check your account?"

"No, why?"

"The check. Mom and Dad got paid."

Jessica scrolls through her phone.
Her eyes turn big.
She is laughing and hugging
Mama Lee in the kitchen.

Dave picks me up and spins
me around a few times. I
am afraid of this height.
I twist and break free
from his arms.

NEW NORMAL

I spend my mornings with Jessica. I nudge her door open and jump on her bed. I wait until she's awake. Then, we walk to the coffee shop.

On one of the streets, shopping carts and small tents block the sidewalk. This doesn't look like the tents we slept in when we went camping in the mountains. These tents are worn out and falling apart. Jessica and I walk around the parked cars and cross the street. A man is resting in front of a building. We pass by him during our morning walks. He waves at me and Jessica. She smiles and waves back.

We get to the coffee shop. Strangers don't walk up and pet me like they used to. These days, they pull their dogs away or cross the street before we can meet. People are waiting in a line, wearing masks. They are staring at their phones and standing far apart. The world outside feels very different.

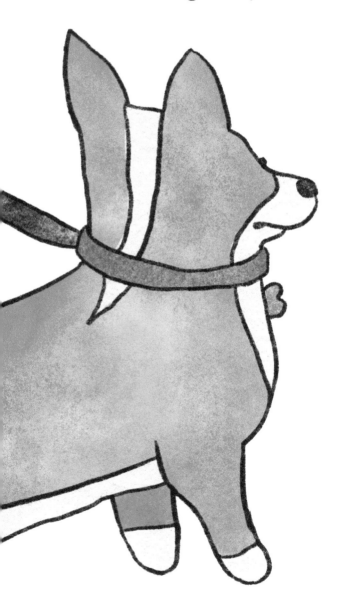

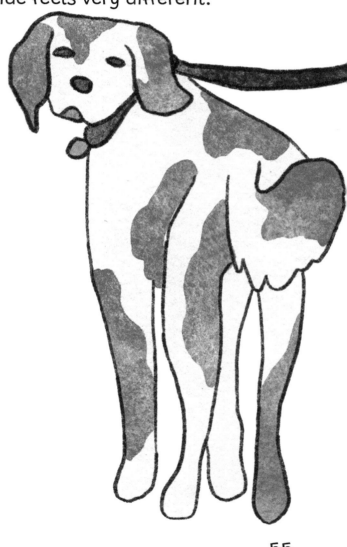

55

It's now the beginning of summer. We start spending more time outdoors as the weather turns warmer. I even saw Homer at the park the other day! I am exploring different places and building new memories with the family.

Dave is finally done with college. We celebrate his graduation at home, in front of the television. He is wearing a gown and a funny looking, square cap on his head. Julie comes over with a gift for Dave and treats for me.

For the next few nights, Jessica is up late writing something. She is very focused, typing away. Her door is open, so I walk up to her desk and nuzzle her leg. Jessica is in a good mood. She picks me up and holds me in her lap. The album is open to the last page. There's a picture of her wearing a mask, holding me. I place my paws on the keyboard.

"Look, Deegee," she says. "I'm writing a story about you."

Joann Song is a young professional living in Los Angeles. She is a graduate of UC San Diego. Her family owned a corgi while growing up in Los Angeles. Currently, she owns a Shiba Inu. She loves dogs and isn't sure how she would've coped during the pandemic without her own.

CPSIA information can be obtained
at www.ICGtesting.com
Printed in the USA
LVHW071403190121
676877LV00017B/612